To my Mom, (Kay) Kennythe Sprau Thomsen, who was a woman as unique as her name. She was a dedicated teacher, always insisting on good grammar and good character. Mom was loved dearly by her family and friends and an inspiration to us all through her wit, humor, and creativity.

WNZ Publications
P.O. Box 393
Mecosta, MI 49332

Paperback: ISBN 0-9656714-6-1
Hardcover: ISBN 0-9656714-8-8
SAN 253-9896

Printed by Custom Printers, Grand Rapids, MI

The FanTom Spider

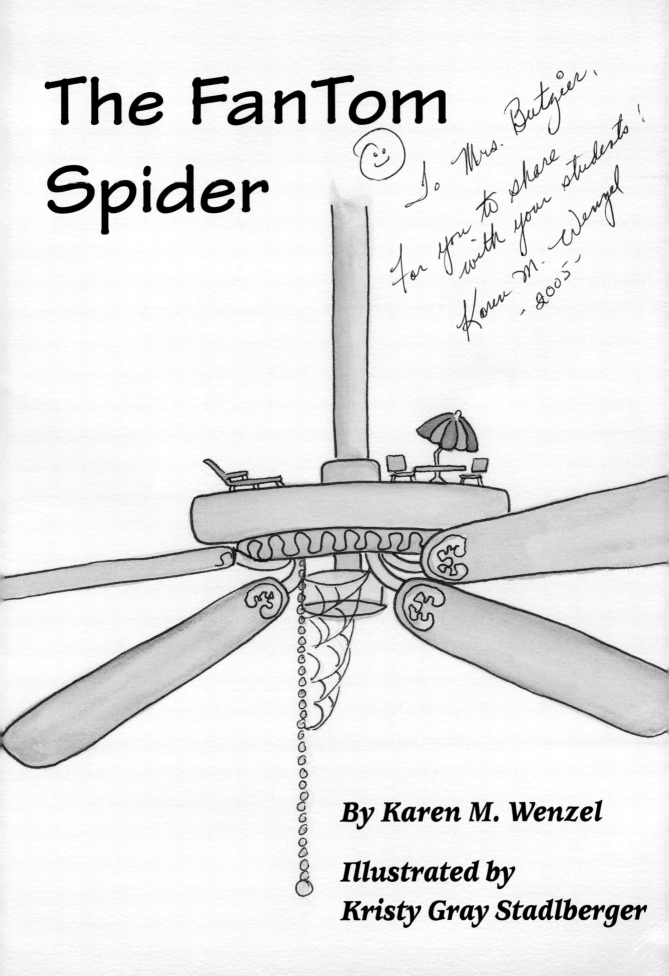

By Karen M. Wenzel

Illustrated by
Kristy Gray Stadlberger

Mr. and Mrs. W. sat in their living room reading. The ceiling fan turned slowly pushing down a cool breeze. Mr. W. glanced up toward the fan. "Mrs. W., the spider has spun another web," he said. "Oh, dear, I dusted it away just yesterday!" said Mrs. W. "Do you think that spider lives in our fan? He is like a PHANTOM SPIDER because we never see him."

"A **PHANTOM SPIDER**," laughed Tom.
He had been listening to Mr. and
Mrs. W. from his cozy apartment
inside the fan. He sat in his lazy spider
chair, watching his favorite TV show
and enjoying a soda and popcorn.

"Perhaps I shall take
a little nap after my
favorite show," said Tom.

Mr. W. finished reading the newspaper, and was taking a short nap in his comfortable chair. A fly buzzing around his head awoke him. He brushed the fly away and thought, "I will use Mrs. W's long-handled feather duster to dust away the spider web!" As Mr. W. dusted the web away, the fan began to **rock** back and forth.

Tom had fallen asleep watching *Spiderella* on TV. All of a sudden he felt a **terrible** jolt. Everything in his apartment went flying. "It must be an **earthquake**!" he said, as his bowl of popcorn flew through the air . . . . "No," he said sadly, "it's only Mr. W. dusting away my web." And he began to clean up his apartment.

Mr. W. put away
the long-handled feather
duster and came back to
the living room with Mrs. W's step stool. Climbing
up to the fan, he peeked in. "I wonder if I can see that
PHANTOM SPIDER inside the fan," he muttered.

Tom heard Mr. 🧩 W. climbing he 🧩 step stool. Through the windows of his 🧩 apartment he saw **TWO BIG EYES** peering at him! He 🧩 flattened himself against the wall, hoping that Mr. W. could not 🧩 see him! "I can't see a **thing**!" said Mr. W., "It's too dark inside the fan." "*Whew!* That was close," said Tom.

Tom spent the night
carefully weaving
another fine web —
inch by inch, down
the chain of the fan.
He thought to himself,
"This certainly can be
a *topsy-turvy* job!"

The next
morning Mr. W.
found Barney, the cat,
looking up   at the
ceiling fan.   "Oh, I don't believe it!"
said Mr.   W. — "**another web**! Did
you see   that PHANTOM SPIDER,
Barney?   We never see him!" Barney
just blinked his eyes and smiled to himself.

"I have an idea," said Mr. W. "This should put an end to these
webs!" He stretched the vacuum hose up to the fan and turned it on.

Tom was resting in his chair after his busy night. A very loud *whirring* sound startled him! All of a sudden he was being pulled toward his windows! His bunny slippers were being ripped from his feet, books went **flying!** Everything in his apartment was being pulled toward the windows! He grabbed the back of his chair and the lamp with four of his eight legs! . . . . and then it stopped. "There," said Mr. W. brushing his hands. "No more spider webs now." And he put away the vacuum cleaner.

After a few minutes Tom peeked cautiously out his windows. Mr. W. was nowhere to be seen. The web was gone and his apartment was a mess again. He felt sad ... And he thought — "Mr. and Mrs. W. don't like my webs but I don't want to move out of my cozy little apartment in the fan." He thought some more — "maybe — just maybe — if I made a beautiful web that *sparkled* ...." That night he began to work, planning and spinning a most beautiful design into a web — the most *beautiful* web he had ever spun. He finished just as the first rays of sunlight came through the window. He said proudly, "That's the **VERY BEST I can do!**"

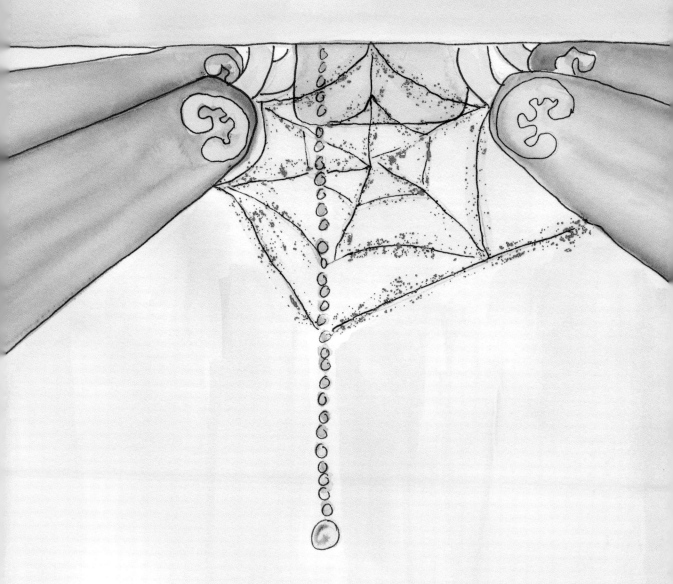

Mr. and Mrs. W. were up early the next morning. "Mrs. W.," shouted Mr. W., "Will you look at this! That persistent little spider has spun **another web** . . . But look how it sparkles in the sun-light. It really is quite beautiful!" "Well," said Mrs. W., "it would be a shame to dust away a web that is so special." "I agree", said Mr. W., "I think we should let our PHANTOM SPIDER live in our fan — but he needs a new name — The FanTom Spider." Tom looked down happily from his patio above his cozy apartment.